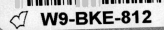

DOWN ON THE FARM

by Merrily Kutner

illustrated by Will Hillenbrand

SCHOLASTIC INC.

New York Toronto London Auckland Sydney
Mexico City New Delhi Hong Kong Buenos Aires

ISBN 0-439-86319-2

Text copyright © 2004 by Merrily Kutner.
Illustrations copyright © 2004 by Will Hillenbrand. All rights reserved.
Published by Scholastic Inc., 557 Broadway, New York, NY 10012,
by arrangement with Holiday House, Inc. SCHOLASTIC and associated
logos are trademarks and/or registered trademarks of Scholastic Inc.

12 11 10 9 8 7 6 5 4 3   17 18 19 20 21

Printed in the U.S.A.   40

First Scholastic printing, February 2006

The text typeface is Hillenbrand Writing.

The artwork was rendered with oils and inks on vellum.

For my precious daughter, Marisa—
in loving memory
M. K.

To Sheri Woodward,
down on the farm
W. H.

Sun comes up.
KiD WaKes uP!
Down on the farm,
DOWN ON THE FARM.

"Rooster, shoo!"
COCK-a-DOODLE-DOO.

Down on the farm,
DOWN ON THE FARM.

Crows peck straw—
CaW, CaW, CaW.
Down on the farm,
DOWN ON THE FARM.

Horses say,
"NaY, NaY, NaY."

Down on the farm,
DOWN ON THE FARM.

Cows will chew—
Moo, Moo, Moo.
Down on the farm,
DOWN ON THE FARM.

SALT LICK

Time for lunch—
CRUNCH. CRUNCH.
CRUNCH.
Down on the farm,
DOWN ON THE FARM.

SALT LICK

"Ducks, come back!"
QUACK. QUACK. QUACK.
Down on the farm,
DOWN ON THE FARM.

Geese kerplonk—
HONK, HONK, HONK.
Down on the farm,
DOWN ON THE FARM.

SALT LICK

Turkeys squabble—
GOBBLE, GOBBLE, GOBBLE.
Down on the farm,
DOWN ON THE FARM.

Dog's on roof—
WOOF, WOOF, WOOF.
Down on the farm,
DOWN ON THE FARM.

Pig snouts point—
OINK. OINK. OINK.
Down on the farm,
DOWN ON THE FARM.

Goats repeat,
"BLEAT, BLEAT, BLEAT."
Down on the farm,
DOWN ON THE FARM.

Sheep graze far—
Baa, Baa, Baa.

Down on the farm,
DOWN ON THE FARM.

Chicks won't sleep—
PEEP. PEEP. PEEP.
Down on the farm,
DOWN ON THE FARM.

Cats powwow—
MeoW. MeoW. MeoW.
Down on the farm,
DOWN ON THE FARM.

Sun goes down.
SHH!
QUIET TOWN.
Down on the farm,
DOWN ON
THE FARM.